College Erotica Bundle

Three Confessions of a Naughty Girl Stories

Ashley Dixon

Contents

My Sister's Boyfriend

I have always thought of myself as a bit of a naughty girl. It is true. I just like to fuck. There is nothing wrong with that. Or there shouldn't be, but being a woman that can firmly state that she enjoys a good dick has always been next to impossible without being called a slut. Well, in that case, I am a slut. Don't believe me? Well, maybe you will change your mind after I tell you what I am about to tell you.

So, this whole thing started after a brief but unbearable period when every dick in town seemed to be purposefully avoiding my vagina. It was as if there had been a drought of cock. I don't know why that happened. I consider myself to be a little above the average gal. I am a 5'7" tall brunette with DD breasts, and I love sucking cock. So, how was I not finding a lovely gentleman to suck off? Anyway, for one reason or another, I wasn't getting any good cock, and it was driving me crazy. During that time, I had to recur to touching myself a lot. Not that I don't enjoy some good ol' self-pleasuring, but nothing can replace the feeling of a thick, living manhood inside. Such was my despair that my good little sister Mia started to worry about me. She is the opposite of me. She has always been the good girl, the perfect daughter to our parents, the golden student, the one that got the prestigious scholarship to get into college and would peel her ass off studying for her exams. Me, not so much. I tried college, but it didn't take much for me to realize that it was just an overly expensive way to get laid off. I will not lie, I really enjoyed being fucked my head off during that time, but those stories I will tell you another time. Going back to where I was: Mia was worried about her spoiled older sister. Although I am just a year older than her, she has always reverenced me as if I was the incarnation of wisdom. I know it sounds as odd to me as probably to you after reading what I have told you so far. This is the thing with younger siblings: they will adore you no matter what.

I said that Mia is the golden girl, and it certainly is compared to me, but that doesn't mean she hasn't fucked yet, even though she has never been married. That is her only little, dirty secret. At least that I know. Our parents would sacrifice themselves for the honor of their virgin daughter to anyone who tried to point out that she is, in fact, no virgin, but let's not bring them here today.

The trouble started on a Friday. But doesn't all trouble always start on Fridays? At least for me, it has mostly been the case. So, this Friday, I was going crazy from "cock-deprivation syndrome." That is how Mia had named my bad streak.

"Erin, you must stop behaving as if not getting fucked a Friday night means the end of the world."

I was certainly bordering on craziness that afternoon. Frantically looking at my phone, expecting someone in my extensive list of fuck-toys would send me a message, a dick pick, something that could ignite the process that would end with my throat full of cum at the end of the night. But nothing was coming that way. Some of them were out of town, others seemed to be already taken for the night, and there were a few with whom things had turned sour.

"It is over, Mia. I will text Anthony." I said.

She screamed.

"The fuck you are! I hereby forbid you to contact that stupid loser," said Mia and took the phone away from my hand.

"Come on! I know he is a douche! But he has a good piece, and I really need to get laid soon, or I will finally lose my mind!"

"No. Not under my watch. It is not only that he is a douchebag, but that he also hurt your feelings. I don't want to be here tomorrow hearing you cry over how that asshole managed to once again screw you over."

"Well," I said, "I may not be crying over Anthony tomorrow, but you will surely have to hear me cry because of having spent another Friday night of my youth with no action."

She probably would not even hear me cry because she used to spend her Saturdays with Danny, her boyfriend. But, nonetheless, she seemed upset because of me.

"Let's try something. Why don't you come out tonight with Danny and me?"

I looked back at her with a bored expression.

"And how would that solve any of my problems?"

"Danny has a lot of hot friends. We could ask him to bring one tonight."

I wasn't expecting that kind of offer coming from Mia. Although we were close, she was extremely jealous about letting me in her private life. She had set strict boundaries as she tried to maintain her little sex adventures with Danny out of sight. Mia knew that with me in the proximity of her boyfriend, I would immediately know they were fucking. And ironically, that was precisely what happened. Until that night, I had a slight suspicion that they were not virgins anymore, but it took me less than ten minutes after being all together in the bar to realize that they were doing it like rabbits. Boring rabbits, I would later learn, but rabbits nonetheless. So yes, that means that I accepted the invitation from Mia. I knew Danny had some hot friends, and to be honest, I was willing to accept even a not-so-hot one if that meant that I was going to finally end the cock-dry-season I was suffering.

And so there we were, the three of us at the bar. Yes, I said three because even though Mia had asked Danny to bring a friend, he had arrived alone.

Upon seeing him coming our way, I looked nervously at my sister.

"Calm down," she told me. "His friend will probably show up later."

But that would not be the case, as he made it clear after greeting us.

"Um, regarding my friend Jake... he is not coming. I am sorry. I asked him to come, and he was all in, but he just called me. It seems that his mother has just had an accident, and he needs to take care of her. I am sorry, ladies. You will have to conform with me alone."

"Oh my god!" said my sister. "Isis Jake's mother going to be fine?"

"Um, yes. At least from what he told me, it was just that she twisted her ankle. But he needs to keep her company tonight, as no one else can help her."

Mia, being the sweetheart that she is, was relieved. Myself? Not so much. Not that I didn't care about the mother's well-being of the guy I intended to fuck that night, but yes, I didn't care about that. I had expected to meet one of Danny's handsome football player friends. Instead, I was stuck between him and my sister in the middle of a horrendous bar. I was about to pack my things and get out when Mia grabbed me by the arm.

"What are you doing?" she whispered into my ear.

"I am leaving. What else can I do? You stay with Danny, and I will see you later. Maybe I can watch a movie at home before falling asleep alone as the loser I have become."

"But you can't just leave!"

"Why not?"

"Because we came together!"

"So what? Your boyfriend can drive you home later."

"I know, but... just stay. Let's make the best of this situation. It is s a sister's night, after all!"

"Yeah, sister's night with your boyfriend."

"I know, I know, but you have to think positively! Maybe you will end up meeting some other handsome guy tonight."

"Is this because you just don't want me to text Anthony or because you don't want to hear me complain tomorrow?"

Mia giggled.

"A little of both."

I was about to continue the discussion but then decided that I could stay there a little more. After all, I had dressed for the occasion with a generous cleavage that was gaining some eyes, and I had spent about an hour putting on makeup. The problem was that the bar was quiet that night, and there weren't many single guys I could see. Most of the gentlemen were with their girls, and the few that seemed single also seemed utterly unimpressed by our presence.

Meanwhile, my sister and her boyfriend were having a boring conversation. I didn't want to spend the entire night surrounded by them, so I told them I would get a cocktail. Of course, my actual intention was to get some dick. I looked around a little but was completely ignored. Where had all those eyes that had been prying on my boobs gone? It was as if they had vanished because the guys just kept ignoring me. I went to the bar counter and asked the barman for a beer. A nice-looking guy was sitting there drinking alone.

"Hi, handsome," I said. He looked back at me and didn't say a word, but he just made a hand gesture to let me know he was not interested. That felt like the ultimate humiliation. I took my beer and returned to the table with Mia and Danny. When I was just a few steps away, I overheard them discussing. Mia was agitated, and I could see she had turned red.

"DON'T DENY IT! I SAW HOW YOU WERE STARING AT MY SISTER'S TITS!" she shouted to him.

He shook his head.

"It is not what you think, Mia," he tried to calm my sister.

"I SAW IT! I KNOW YOU LIKE HER! YOU HAVE ALWAYS WANTED TO FUCK HER!" now my sister started crying.

Danny saw me standing a few feet from them. I felt uncomfortable and aroused at the same time. I had always kept my dirty thoughts away from my sister's boyfriend, but he was indeed a nice-looking man. He, too, was part of the football team playing quarterback and had a nicely compact body. And yes, a rounded ass that I have indeed noticed. Now I was thinking about his dick. Would he have a thick, solid cock? Judging by my taste in men and considering the shared genetics with my sister, I was sure that if she had settled with a man, it was because of a very long reason. I mean, good reason.

My sister noticed Danny was not looking at her anymore. Instead, he was now fixated on me. His eyes directly posed over my cleavage in a lustful gaze. It was like when you are found doing something nasty, like picking your nose, and you try to deny it, but at the same time, something in your brain makes you do it even more. He was in the same situation. Just staring like an idiot at my boobs. Finally, my sister realized he was not listening to her anymore and followed his eyes until she saw me. That was it. She was hysterical.

"See?! See?! You are disgusting!" she said and stood up. She approached me and grabbed me by the arm before telling me we were leaving.

"But I thought you said you wanted us to spend the night here. So I was just checking on the guys."

"Please, take me home. I cannot stay here anymore."

I complied, and we went outside the bar.

"I think it is over," she finally said when we got into the car, "I mean between Danny and me." I started driving.

"But why?" I asked, playing dumb.

"Danny is... he is just not my type."

"He was until tonight," I replied.

"Haven't you noticed? Since he arrived, he couldn't stop looking at you. It was just like a filthy animal, drooling over the sight of your tits."

I knew that was a particularly thorny topic for Mia. She has nice tits, don't get me wrong. It is just that they are not as flashy as mine. She is just a B cup, and while there are plenty of men who like or even prefer girls with small boobs, more of them like their girls with big tits like mine.

"You are being way too harsh with the man. All guys look at other girls' boobs. It is in their nature."

Mia started to cry.

"You don't understand," she said, sobbing. "I think she has been cheating on me! And what happened tonight all but confirmed it!"

I wanted to grab her head under my arms and tell her everything would be fine.

"Why didn't you tell me this before?"

"It is just that I cannot be sure! It has been driving me crazy for the last months, and now, seeing how he stared at you… that was the moment I realized I was right about my suspicion."

We arrived home.

"Well, we are here. Go to sleep and think a little more about this, will you? You might have just got everything wrong."

We got out of the car and went straight inside and to our rooms. I felt exhausted. While I hadn't ended the night the way I was hoping, all the drama with Mia had drained me completely. I was so exhausted that I let myself fall into the bed without even undressing. I just didn't have the strength. I was there, trying to forget everything that had happened that night when I heard behind the flimsy wall that separates my room with Mia's her phone ringing. She answered, and I could hear the following discussion. It didn't take much time to realize that she and Danny were over. She screamed and shouted and cried, accused him of cheating, and from what I could piece together, he didn't deny it. That was it. I wondered if they would have ended things if I hadn't been there that night. If he had looked at other girl's tits instead. Because the fact was that he had been gazing at my tits. It was obvious that it had taken part in the situation. I fell asleep and woke up on Saturday at noon. I stretched and grabbed my phone.

I had a message from Danny. Well, that was something I was indeed not expecting. I read it through. He wanted to talk to me. He didn't even mention Mia in the message. It was as if they had never been together, much less broken up. So, I texted him back, asking what he wanted to talk. I waited a few moments, and nothing happened. I went outside of my room and checked for Mia. She wasn't at home. I figured she would have gone out with some of her friends. She would have a lot to talk about what an asshole Danny had ended up being.

I stared at the phone and nothing. I felt a little stupid and tried to forget about it. I dressed and went to the kitchen to cook a good breakfast. I grabbed some eggs and was about to crack them when I received a text from Danny. He was asking me if I could go see him. He wanted to "talk" about "things." Just that. I thought about the idea for a minute. I was sure Mia would not want me to go see her now ex. Much less after everything that took place and how it became clear that I probably played some role in them breaking up. But at the same time, I was intrigued by the proposal and, to be honest, a little flattered to think that Danny had been looking at me. So, I told him yes, and he said he was coming for me in fifteen minutes. I finished my breakfast quickly and put up some makeup before he arrived. I went inside his car, and he drove us to a nearby park.

We sat on a bench. The weather was sunny and warm. We looked at each other, and then he finally said,

"Thank you for coming. I just wanted to talk with you because of all that happened last night. "

"You and Mia broke up, right?"

"Yeah, she was the one that broke with me."

"I am sorry."

"She said that I couldn't stop looking your way."

"I know. She said the same to me."

"Well... she is not wrong."

"What do you mean?"

"I don't know how to say this... but... it is just that you are a beautiful woman. And it is true. I couldn't stop staring at your incredible boobs last night. But don't mind me. I shouldn't be saying this."

I blushed.

"If that's the case, tell me why you wanted to meet with me."

"I don't know. It was probably a stupid idea. I first thought I could talk you into trying to convince your sister to take me back. But I see you again here, under the sun, looking so gorgeous... I can't help but tell you how you make me feel."

"Well, yes. It was a stupid idea. That is for sure. But at the same time... you know, I also find you attractive."

I quickly glanced at his crotch and saw it was clearly getting some heat.

"You meant it?"

"Yes, for sure. You are a handsome man. If it wasn't because of my sister, I would totally fuck you."

Danny was getting nervous; I could tell because of how he was now moving in his seat.

"Please, don't tell me that. You know, I really like Mia. It is only that she is so... I don't know how to put it... puritanical?"

I laughed.

"What do you mean? I know you two have done it!"

"Yes, we did it sometimes, but she is boring. Always the same, old, and tried missionary. She never blew me. She doesn't want anybody to know that we have fucked. It makes me look kind of bad with the boys."

"Oh, poor Danny," I said while gently touching his face.

"Meanwhile, you..."

"What about me?"

"Well, don't take it badly, but stories are going around. They say that you are the complete opposite of your sister."

"How so?"

"There are stories about you being wild."

"I will not admit nor deny them, but given the circumstances, maybe you could test them yourself."

I was being my sluttiest slut. I admit it. But to be honest, this guy was not good for Mia. She deserved something better. To that, I could agree. And my thought process went that if I sucked the guy's dick, my sister would have been absolutely right about leaving him. So that was it.

Danny looked at me once again. This time, his face had changed to a lustful grin.

"You know, my parents are not home right now."

"What are you suggesting?" I always liked to play a little dumb. Guys really love dumb bitches. Just a little to make them say out loud what is implied.

"Want to come? I would really love to put those stories to the test."

"I don't know," I said and waited a few seconds to enjoy Danny's mounting excitement. "What about Mia?"

"Forget her. I don't think we were good for each other after all."

To that, I could agree.

"Well, in that case...."

We went straight back to his car and then to his basement, which was surprisingly tidier than I had imagined for a man his age and average intelligence. Anyway, I wasn't there to judge him by his brains but by his crotch. The second we arrived, he closed the door behind us and took off his shirt. I wasn't wrong: he had a nice six-pack with well-rounded pectorals. He started kissing me. He smelled of expensive citric perfume and manhood. I grabbed him by his shoulders and pushed him towards me until I got stuck between him and the wall. I could feel his bulge pressing against my abdomen. I bit his lips, and he responded by biting mine while undressing me from the top. I wanted to see if his shaft was what I was expecting. I went under his pants until I could feel it. There it was, palpitating and erected, hard as an iron rod. I could only think about getting it inside me. It had been so long since I had a good fuck, and now, I was finally going to get it from my sister's ex. He dropped his pants and was now fully naked.

"Do you want me to fuck you?" he asked, knowing the answer precisely.

"Yes," I supplicated.

"But first, you are going to suck me off."

"Yes, whatever you say."

He forced me to the ground until I was on my knees, at which point he grabbed my head and offered me his thick cock. I swallowed it whole and then began to lick it. He had his hands on my hair and was rocking my head from side to side while he did it.

"You are a dirty slut, aren't you?"

I felt an ardor going through my entire body and my pussy flooding with wetness. I was grabbing his cock with my left hand while still sucking it. I then took my right hand to my lower lips and frantically touched them, getting closer to the clit. I wanted to suck him dry, but I also wanted to get pussy-fucked. I could feel his delicious pre-cum making its way into my mouth, and I could also sense his cock approaching the point where it would split all his precious load. I then slowed the pace of my sucking and looked into his eyes. He understood and took my head off his dick.

"Get up. I want to see you naked now."

I complied with the request and undressed.

"You really have a nice pair," he said, looking at my tits as if he couldn't believe his luck.

"Why don't you taste them?"

He further pushed me to the wall and went down to cup my nipples with his mouth. I grabbed him by his hair while he sucked and bit my nubs. He was like a feral animal, urged by his primal instinct to fuck me. I was sure he hadn't learned all those moves with my puritanical sister. And now I also could understand why he had been so keen to get into my pants. I moaned as he took his hands to my tits, massaging them while still eating my nipples.

Oh, Danny!" I whispered, feeling my pussy titling with excitement, ready to receive his hard-on. He then started to lick the sides of my nipples, moving through my tits as if they were a forbidden, delicious fruit. He moved down with his tongue until reaching the apex of my thighs. He then got down on his knees, spread my legs apart, and pressed his tongue against my lips, coming close to my clitoral hood. He proceeded in a calm but steady manner until he reached my clit, all the while letting his face soak up my juices. He licked it gently at first and then started to increase the pressure. I was gasping for air, squeezing his hair. My legs started to tremble, and he took it as a hint to pull out, leaving me eager to feel all of his cock inside me.

"You taste just as good as your sister. It must run in the family," he said.

"I want you to fuck me where you took Mia's virginity," I replied.

He took me by the hips and walked me to a desk full of comic books and toys that he pulled out with his arm. I turned around, giving him a full display of my thick ass that he grabbed with both hands and squeezed until I felt a delicious wave of pain.

"Fuck me now," I murmured.

Danny spread my legs while I was still standing, leaning against the desk, and he entered his hard dick into my tight, wet pussy. I don't know if it was because it had been a long time since I had had one inside or the particular shape of his penis. Still, it felt much bigger once he was inside than I had seen and felt in my mouth minutes ago. He started pumping my pussy from behind like it was the last time he would ever fuck in his entire life. I cried for more as he continued the drill until I felt that my pussy was getting tighter, contracting around his cock. I arched my back and exploded in a large moment of agony that shook my entire body.

He continued as if nothing had happened. He still was to come. But I had a different plan.

"I want you to cum on my tits," I said, knowing how much he fancied them.

Danny pulled out and said no word but grabbed me by the hips and turned me around to face him again. He pushed me back to my knees and put his big, venous cock inside my mouth. It tasted salty, a mix of his pre-cum and my own juices. That drove me further crazy, and I sensed how my pussy was getting wetter as if I hadn't just come. I took my hand back to my clit and started slamming it again while sucking his dick until I sensed he was about to cum. I took it out of my mouth and stroked it a few times until I saw his facial muscles contract and his entire body shake as if he was about to collapse. Then, he fired off a massive load of spunk that landed on my tits. It was warm and sticky. I swiped a finger through it, looking at him in the eyes, I put it inside my mouth and smiled.

"You are such a cumslut," he said, still recovering.

I didn't answer. I grabbed his balls and massaged them. I didn't want to let him go until I dried his sack completely.

"What are you doing?"

"Is that all you got?"

"You want more? I will give you more." He grabbed my head once more, and this time I was prepared to receive his cock, which by this point had lost some of its potency. I knew I had to work hard to regain its full glory again, so I sucked with passion, stroking it with my hand until it started to wake up again. I sucked, increasing the pace and stroking my pussy as hard as possible. He then moaned, and I knew it was time for the second load that filled my mouth with even more sperm. I swallowed it all, and he then tried to pull out, but I wouldn't let him and kept stroking him until I came, just when I had completely depleted his balls. He then tried to pull out again; this time, I let him.

"Do you have a towel?" I asked him. I was such a mess. Cum all over my tits and stomach.

He looked around for something I could use to clean myself, and his eyes fixed on a spot in his bedroom.

"Your sister left one of her panties here last time. Would that do it?"

I smiled and extended my hand to receive my sister's panties. I passed it through my tits, taking care of getting every little spill of cum, and then gave it back to him.

"I assume you will want to keep that."

He grinned and took it from my hand.

We started to get dressed in silence.

I could sense he was worried about something.

"What is it?" I asked him.

"What?" he looked confused.

"Something is bothering you, right?"

"Erin, today was incredible...."

"Yeah, I know... but we can't repeat it because of my sister and all that. Right? Is this what you are thinking?"

"Well..."

"I understand."

"It is like... If only one of you could have what the other has. Maybe if you were as lovely as Mia and if Mia was as wild in bed as you...."

I laughed hard.

"You enjoyed fucking me like crazy precisely because I am not as lovely and pure as Mia. And it is fine. You like her because of how she is as well. Maybe you two should try to reconsider getting back together," I said, and I finished dressing.

"Yes, maybe you are right."

We didn't say a word on the way back to my home, and when we arrived, he asked me not to tell Mia about what had happened between us.

"You don't have anything to worry about," I said, getting off his car.

Mia wasn't home yet, and I felt relieved. I needed to take a shower. I wonder if she could recognize the smell of Danny in me. When she got later that day, she was already starting to regret the breakup. She had spent the day talking with her best friend, Natalie, who had convinced her she had overreacted. I didn't say anything.

A week later, Mia and Danny were back together, and she never suspected what had happened between him and me. He and I crossed paths one time. He came to pick Mia up to go to the movies, and we acted as if we barely knew each other. It was fine by me. While I had really enjoyed fucking him that afternoon, my bad streak was over, and I was having a lot of sexy adventures. What's that? Do you want me to tell you about those other savage sex sessions I enjoyed? You will have to wait until we meet again. Until then, warm kisses wherever you most want!

My Oral Test

Have I talked about my time in college yet? I wasn't your typical "A" student, nor I ended with a 4.0 GPA when I was finished. I think that should go without saying. However, I can assure you that I learned some valuable lessons. Everybody knows that college is that crazy time in your life when you pass half of the time wasted and the other half fucking like there is no tomorrow. I always preferred the part of fucking, so I would say, for me, it was a time of 100% learning. Learning about sucking cock and all the sexual positions imaginable more than anything else but learning in the end.

Today I would like to tell you about how I gave Mark, the virgin, his first blowjob ever. He was a nerdy guy in my Spanish class. He always seemed severe in class and eager to answer questions from the professor. I really didn't like him much at first. He wore a pair of ugly, squared glasses covering most of his face and talked little besides answering the professor's questions. Even worst, whenever he would speak with another classmate because the professor had given us an exercise to complete in small groups or something similar, he would only do it using the Spanish language. I mean, give me a break! The fact that the class was full of guys like Mark made it all the worst. However, without a doubt, what was really difficult to grasp was that the class ran on Fridays from six to eight in the afternoon. What was I thinking when I enrolled? Who knows? I might as well have been too wasted to stop for a second to see the mistake I was making when I enrolled. I did need the course to graduate, and in RateMyProfessor.com, there was a consensus that the Prof was accessible, and the course itself required little effort to get a passing grade. But boy, had I overestimated my ability to endure such a bore on Fridays.

The first months really put me to the test. I was completely lost, unable to understand what all those sexy-sounding words meant, unable to remember the overly complicated Spanish verb tenses. And don't even get me started on the difference between the verbs "Ser" and "Estar." To make things worse, people assumed that I already knew how to speak the language just because my last name means "Moon" in Spanish. Even though I have a Hispanic heritage from my father's side, he never spoke to me in Spanish, and the times my sister and I would travel to Latin America to meet our family there, they would mainly communicate with us in English. So yes, I was basically at the same beginner level as the rest of the class.

The only thing that kept me going was that I knew that when the class finished, it was the official start of the weekend. But during the winter months, that wasn't consolation enough. I would just get out of class, get into my on-campus room, and stay inside until Monday. It was just depressing.

Things took a turn for the unexpected on a Tuesday. I was in college for a PoliSci course when I crossed paths in a hallway with Mark, who was coming the opposite way. I recognized him immediately. It was almost impossible to miss the guy with his slender figure and pimpled face, always carrying an array of books under his arm and dressed as if he was one of the professors, one ugly and old professor for what matters. I said "Hi" because I can be a lot of kinds of bitch, but an uneducated bitch I am not. He almost came to a complete stop and mumbled something I could barely hear. He seemed surprised that I had recognized him and also a little excited. It was not his fault: I used to attend the PoliSci class wearing the sluttiest clothes I could without being called out by some college's authority. Of course, that was because I was trying my best to seduce the professor in that class, but that is a story for another time. So, there I was, wearing a cleavage that let almost nothing to imagination although it was the end of January, wearing makeup as if I was about to go to a party and all smiles to this nerdy guy who I barely knew.

In case you still don't know, I honestly have great tits. I am not afraid to state the facts as they stand; in this instance, I will do that. I'm a 34 double-D, and I try to show as much of them as possible. I love how guys freak out when I make them bounce in front of their eyes. The fact that most of them would kill for a chance to submerge their faces in my boobs or put their cocks between them for a ride, but only a few lucky ones will ever be able to do so, turns me on. I could tell that day that Mark was one of those guys who would kill his mother for the privilege of grabbing and kissing my tits, eating my nips, and whatever else was going through his nerdy mind at the time.

After saying "Hi" to him, I went about my business as if nothing had happened because nothing had. I had no control over how this poor creature reacted to a girl talking to him. I went into my class, and after it finished, I met Julia to have lunch in the cafeteria. We used to meet every Tuesday's noon to have something to eat. Still, it was mostly just to talk about the boys we were fucking at the moment, the boys we were planning to fuck, and the boys we had recently fucked.

Julia likes dick as much as I do. However, she has higher standards than me. While I will fuck almost any guy I come across if I am desperate, Julia takes much more consideration in deciding who she fucks. For instance, I know for a fact that she once rejected a guy when they were both undressed and ready to boink just because the guy had a relatively small dick of about 5 inches. In that case, I would have taken it as it came. I have a certain kink for small-dick men, but I also have a kink for big-dick men, so I could just say I have a kink for dicks.

Julia saw me coming and pointed at the empty seat she had reserved for me. She had already brought something to eat, so I went to where my friend was and sat.

"Well, hello you! I assume you had a class with Professor Peck, right?"

I blushed a little.

"You say because of this?" I said, taking a hand to my chest.

"Why else?"

"Well, yes, I attended Professor Peck-er's class," I giggled.

"You dirty slut. How is that going?"

"Well," I said, sipping a coke, "I can't say it is going how I expected."

"What do you mean?"

"He seems to not have noticed me at all."

"Are you insane? Look at you, bitch. How could a man not notice you with those round, jumping balloons you are practically showing to anyone who stumbles with you?"

"I know! And that is why it is so frustrating!"

Julia gave her sandwich a tiny bite and then quickly sipped his diet Sprite. I knew that was probably all she was going to have for lunch.

"Have you tried asking him questions after the class?"

"Tried that. No results so far."

"Have you gone to his office hours?"

"Checked. Yes. I did that too. I was dressed as a good escort. Nothing. He barely looked at my body. He focused on my eyes and didn't even glance over my cleavage."

"Well, that is strange, for sure. I mean, look at you. If I was into girls, I would absolutely suck your pussy."

I giggled again.

"I would absolutely love that. Maybe another day?"

"Yes, definitely," said Julia. We used to joke around about sucking each other's pussy and playing with some toys, but so far, we hadn't tried it. "That only leaves one answer to this enigma: he is into guys."

"No," I said confidently. "I know for a fact that he likes women. Last year he fucked Iliona Zervas. Everybody talked about that for months."

"WHAT?" said Julia with her eyes coming out of her sockets.

"You are telling me you never heard?"

"Iliona? The exchange girl from Greece?"

"That one. Yes. Nice Mediterranean olive skin, small tits, though."

"In that case, maybe he is just into skinny girls. And in that case, you would definitely not fit his bill."

"You know which kind of people also are usually flat on their chests?"

We laughed together.

"Oh my god, you are going to kill me, Erin."

"Anyway," I looked at my watch. I needed to get going. "Are you going to tell me about you? What has been with you this week?"

"Long story. Do you have time?"

"I certainly not. I am sorry," I said, genuinely disappointed; Julia's stories were always exciting. "I must get going. By the way, you know who did stare at me as if I was a Picasso painting when we came around in the hallway earlier today?"

"No, who?"

"This nerdy guy that is in my Spanish class, Mark Bowden. I think you and him shared a class last semester."

Julia tried to remember.

"I don't recall."

"You know, thin guy, pimpled face, always trying to outsmart everybody in class?"

"Oh, yes, now I remember! What about him?"

"Nothing in particular," I said as I got up and picked up my books. "I just crossed paths with him in the hallway a moment ago and said hello. He came to a full stop and whispered something that I assumed was a hello or something like that. He did inspect my curves."

"I bet he did! You know that guy's an incel, right?"

"What do you mean?"

"An incel, an involuntary celibate. A guy who would love to fuck but can't get any woman to touch him."

I had never heard the term before. As I said before, I will fuck almost anyone. I don't see the point of restraining myself from doing something so pleasurable and fun.

"You really think the man can't get pussy?"

"Well," she doubted, "I don't really know the guy that much. I mean, we were in this course together, and he looked like a complete tool to me. He was always trying to grab the professor's attention, answering every question and making disapproving noises when other classmates would try to say something. He really thinks of himself as a genius, I think. And usually, these are the guys who can't get pussy. So, there you go. He is either an incel or a virgin. That is for sure."

"Well, maybe I can change that!" I said, letting out a silly laugh.

"You can't control it, can you?"

"I will see you later!" I said and took off.

Julia was right, though. Now that she had told me Mark was probably a virgin, my interest in him grew. Something about taking a guy's virginity has always excited me. You see, taking a guy's virginity is ensuring he will never forget you. No matter what happens, you will forever be part of their personal history. A man can fuck a thousand women after his first bang, and he will probably forget about most of those. Still, he will never forget the woman who took his penis for the first time. And along with that comes adoration and a form of submission that never fails to turn me on.

I left the dinner thinking about taking Mark's virginity. During my following class, I could barely concentrate. I started to feel my pussy getting soaked. What was happening to me? It never ceases to amaze me how much of a whore I am. The class I was in, Introductory Psychology, was soporific, and I could not concentrate. Instead, I was feeling an unstoppable need to get fuck really hard. I looked at the classroom, trying to see if one of my usual fucktoys was there. It was one big room, and I had a hard time figuring out everyone sitting there, but then I saw Shaun. He was an okay guy. We had fucked a few times, nothing fancy. Medium size dick, but otherwise clean and discreet, which was just what I was looking for at that moment. It wasn't that I was looking for a long engagement, just a quick fuck in the washroom. I looked at him until he noticed me. He was several rows closer to the dais where the professor stood, giving his best to educate us. I finally got Shaun's attention. I smiled at him; he smiled back, and I raised my hand to my face in the air and made a blowjob gesture at him. He moved nervously in his seat. I got up and walked out of the classroom into the hallway. It took him less than a minute to join me.

"What do you have in mind now, Erin?" he asked me, but I didn't answer. I just started walking towards a washroom that was used mainly by faculty. It was great for what I had in mind because it was an individual stall and almost hidden behind a corner. Shaun followed me as I entered, and I closed and locked the door after him. I jumped on him like a feral animal and kissed his lips while unbuttoning my shirt. I could immediately sense his hard-on pressing against me. He started to get undressed. The washroom was clean, but it still smelled awful, which only excited me.

"You are such a filthy whore!" said Shaun.

"Shut up and fuck me," I told him, grabbing his pulsing dick as if it was a lollypop.

I sat on the basin, spread my legs, spitted on my palm, and stroked my pussy with it. I didn't need that as I was already a sopping wet mess. He pushed his unprotected shaft inside me. I grabbed him by his buttocks to force him deeper into me.

"Are you going to fill me with your cum?" I whispered in his ear as he started pumping me.

"You are completely insane, Erin Luna."

"Just fuck me like an animal," I said.

I could sense he was enjoying himself, and I was also sure he would go out and tell his friends the second we finished. That only incremented my excitement.

He moved so hard into me that the sink felt like it was coming down. I didn't care. All I wanted was his cum filling my cunt. And then someone tried to open the door. Thankfully, I had locked it. I am so tired of people entering a washroom with its door closed before even knocking.

"Just a second!" I screamed while I pushed Shaun from his buttocks further into me. While his dick was just average, he knew some good moves. I felt as if my pussy was on fire, a raging inferno devouring my entire lower body.

"Shall we get out?" asked Shaun, a little worried.

"Just keep it. Keep fucking me."

And he did with a renewed push that shook my body to the point that I had to hold on to the faucets to keep myself from falling to the floor.

I started to cum when he told me he was also about to cum.

"Impregnate me," I said.

"Are you sure?"

"I want to feel your hot, thick sperm inside me," I said.

With a final pump that almost threw me from the sink, he finally let his explosion of sperm inside me. He leaned against the mirror. I could see he was feeling a little dizzy as if he had left a sizeable chunk of his energy inside my pussy.

"That was so hot," he said.

"Now get the fuck out of here," I responded.

He took his clothes and dressed quickly while I did the same and fixed my makeup. Shaun exited the washroom. The person waiting outside was ready to enter, but he stopped her.

"It is still occupied."

"How is that? This is a single-person washroom," I heard the woman say in an exasperated tone.

I took a little while to finish grooming myself to a respectable standard before exiting the washroom, much to the chagrin of the old hag waiting outside.

"Sorry for that!" I said blamelessly.

I went back to my class, leaving behind the angry faculty.

The rest of the day passed much more relaxed. That washroom fuck was exactly what I needed to forget the sudden excitement that had taken hold of my brain since I got the idea of taking Mark Bowden's virginity.

The rest of the week until the following Friday when I was to meet Mark again, I couldn't help but think about him. To be honest, I didn't find him attractive at all, except for the fact that he had a penis under his pants. That was enough. I didn't need much else. So, when the time finally came, I went to class wearing one of my slutty outfits, one that I would wear for Prof. Peck-er, and sat down next to him in the front row. He saw me coming, and I could tell he was into it because his eyes were fixated on my jugs.

"Is this seat taken?" I asked him casually and took a seat before he could even answer.

I could sense he was starting to feel anxious about having me there. He murmured something I could not hear and saw how his hands started sweating.

"What a boring class this is, right?" I said, just as the professor entered the classroom.

"I am sorry you find this class not to your expectations, Miss Luna," said the professor. I immediately regretted having said that.

"I am sorry, Professor Salazar. Don't take it personally. It is just that it is Friday. It is difficult to concentrate. Nothing wrong with the Spanish, though."

He didn't answer me and started with the lesson.

"That was close," I whispered to Mark, who looked the other way.

It was as if I wasn't there for the rest of the class. He totally ignored me, and I started to feel frustrated. What was with that guy? He answered all the questions as usual and worked alone on the exercises the professor gave us. I tried luring him into a conversation a few more times, saying whatever came to mind out loud, but he ignored me. I was confused. He had seemed pretty excited at the sight of my tits, but it was as obvious that he wasn't engaging with any of my tricks to start a conversation.

When the class ended, he quickly took his books and laptop and walked away without saying or looking back at me. I was feeling very frustrated. That night, we went out with Julia for some drinks, and I told her what had just happened.

"I told you that this guy is a weirdo."

"I know," I said, feeling discouraged. "It is just that I really wanted to get to know him a little better."

"Why? Why did you feel that urge? He is a loser. Let him go die alone, as he is destined to do."

"You are so harsh, Julia! I am curious about him! I don't know. I think everybody deserves a little love."

"Not these guys. They are weirdos. There is something rotten in their brains."

"I refuse to accept what you are saying. I will show you that Mark is not brain rotten. He might be a little introverted and shy, but I am sure he is a good guy."

"Fine, but when you finish with this new whim of yours, don't come back at me crying about how I was right and how you should have just let him alone, playing with his video games as he is probably doing right now."

The next Friday, I went even sluttier than the Friday before, wearing a short dress that exposed my legs and tightened my butt and tits in the most provocative cleavage I could find that wouldn't get me expelled from college. I sat next to Mark again, who looked at me extensively and started sweating from his hands to my sight like the other day.

"Hello, Mark," I said.

"Hello," he said timidly.

Well, that was a triumph considering how things have been so far!

"How are you doing today? Are you excited about our class?"

The professor entered the room, looked at me from toe to head, clicked his tongue while gesturing his incredulity, and started the class. And that was it. I had lost Mark again, as he didn't communicate with me any further for the rest of the class. Once all was over, he took his things and left without even saying goodbye. This was getting ridiculous. At the same time, I would not give Julia the upper hand in this. I'd prove to her that I was correct and that Mark wasn't a weirdo; he just lacked some social skills.

The following Tuesday, when I met her, she laughed at my face.

"I TOLD YOU! It is fine, Erin. Just let this one go. You can't have them all, you know."

I was so angry that she was having a field day with my failure that I felt like punching her in the face, but I calmed down and said,

"I don't want to have them all. But when I want a guy, I get it. That is how it always has been, and I will not allow a virgin to be the first to ruin my record."

"It seems like you are not getting into fucking this semester. Either with Prof Peck or the virgin guy."

"I hope you're having a good time at my expense right now because I'm about to turn things around again, and by the end of the day, I'd have added two names to my list."

"Mark my words: you will not fuck Mark Bowden. Better assume it and move on."

Aside from dick, nothing is more personal to me than a challenge. And Mark had become my most tough challenge so far. I was going to prove Julia wrong.

For the following Friday, I tried something different. Instead of going dressed as a whore, I went like any other casual day when I wasn't trying to bring the attention of men to me. I arrived ten minutes earlier to the class that day, perfect timing to sit next to Mark, who was alone in the classroom.

"Hello, Mark,"

"Hello, Erin,"

So now he knew my name, at least.

"Can I ask you a question, Mark?"

"For sure,"

He talked like a robot, but at least he was now engaging in conversation.

"Why do you seem to avoid talking to me every Friday when we meet?"

He started sweating and stuttering.

"I... I... I just want to pass the class with a good grade. And... and... and you..."

"And me?"

"Don't t-take it personally, but you don't have a good fame."

So that was it? My fame? I already knew what other girls were saying behind my back about how their boyfriends looked at me. I had also fucked some of them, which some women seem to can't stand. I may not be the best at learning Spanish, but I did pick up an expression from a lover I had when I went to Buenos Aires: "hermanas de leche." It literally translates as "cum sisters" which I believe is a far better term than "Eskimo sisters" to describe two ladies who have slept with the same guy in the past. I have a long list of non-biological sisters; you can bet on that. I am even "cum sister" to my actual sibling, but that is a story I have already told*.

Going back to that Friday, I finally got Mark to talk to me. Of course, I laughed when he mentioned my celebrity.

"Don't worry, I don't bite. At least if you don't want me to bite."

"Oh no, no. I don't want you to bite me," he hurried to say.

"Then, nothing to worry about, right?"

"Right. It is just that, again, don't take it the wrong way, but I cannot talk to you in English during the Spanish class. Professor Salazar would notice."

"Then why don't we go to one of the back rows?"

He shook his head.

"No way. I want to be in the front row so that I can hear the explanations."

The classroom started to pack, and Professor Salazar came in to cut all the fun again.

Mark didn't want to talk in English during the class? Well, there was another way that didn't involve speaking. I took out a notepad, scrapped a page, and wrote:

"IF YOU DON'T WANT PROFESSOR SALAZAR TO HEAR YOU SPEAK MAYBE WE CAN PASS ON MESSAGES LIKE THIS AS IF WE STILL WERE IN HIGH SCHOOL"

He took it, read it, and put it down with a smile. It was yet not sufficient, but it was something. The class dragged as usual, and I became impatient again. So I wrote another note and passed it to Mark:

"SO? YOU ARE SUPPOSED TO ANSWER ME" I drew a small heart at the top. Maybe that would melt his shyness a little. He grabbed it and held it in his hand without reading it for a moment that seemed to never end. Finally, he looked at it, read it, and scribbled something before passing me the paper back to me.

I read:

"What do you want to talk about?"

I wrote:

"I WANT TO SUCK YOUR DICK UNTIL YOUR BALLS ARE DRY" and passed it to him, who waited until Professor Salazar's sight moved to another student before reading it. He then read it. I looked directly at him. I wanted to see the expression on his face. He went utterly red and looked the other way. Watching him in the eyes, I licked my lips. He took off his seat and went out of the classroom. That I hadn't expected. In the entire time I've known him, I've never seen him leave a class before it was finished. A few minutes later, he was back, looking relaxed again. He sat in his chair and said nothing. Even worst, he wasn't scribbling anything back to me! I waited and waited, and then the class was over. He took his things and got out as if he was in a hurry. I couldn't believe it! I had been extremely direct about my intentions with him, and he had just left me with empty hands and a dry throat!

"I told you. That guy is a total freak," said to me Julia that night over the phone. "Are you finally ready to move over? It is fine. You cannot win all the battles. There will be some guys who just don't want to fuck you."

"I refuse to accept it."

"Come on, you are being just silly now. Why do you think every man in the world owes you his cum?"

"I don't! It is just that I know Mark wants to fuck me! I saw it in how he looked at my body and blushed when we spoke!"

"Well, maybe he likes the idea of fucking you, but like many other men, when he gets confronted with the chance, he just chickens. His dick won't get hard. It can happen."

"Julia, I can assure you that this is not the case. He took off the class when I passed him the last piece of paper telling him I wanted to suck his dick."

"So?"

"Well, he has never done that before. He never leaves the classroom before it is finished."

"And what does this tell you?"

"He was away for a few minutes, and then he came back looking more relaxed. I would say, even relieved."

Julia went into silence for a second.

"Are you implying that he…"

"I am sure he went to the washroom and jerked off."

"Oh my god, that is so gross!"

"Yes, I know. I mean, it's still exciting to know that it was something I said that prompted him to wank, but I would have preferred if he had let me handle the situation."

"Erin, my girl, I will tell it once more so that you can forget all this: you will not fuck Mark Bowden. Get over it. He is just out of your league. Out of the league of any woman."

"We will see."

Next time I saw Mark was again on a Tuesday afternoon when I was on my way to the PoliSci class. I saw him talking with some other random dude in one hallway. He seemed so passionate and confident. Not like when I was around. So, an idea struck me. I was, of course, wearing a very provocative dress that barely covered my tits. I went his way, acting casual and pretending I didn't know him. He saw me coming in his direction and continued talking with this other guy. He was leaning against the wall, and his friend was in front of him, so when I walked past them, he couldn't see me, but I made sure Mark could. At that precise moment, when I was walking around them and saw that Mark was looking at me from the corner of his eye, I flashed him my boobs. No one else was in the hallway then, and the only person who could see was him. I then blew him a kiss and went my way.

I was very excited about meeting him that Friday but, to the surprise of everybody, including the professor, he didn't show up. Was I to blame? The situation was getting ridiculous. Never had I begged a guy to fuck me. I was beginning to understand how some men feel when they appear unable to get pussy and turn slightly insane.

That night when I told Julia, she laughed.

"Do you see it? You can see the irony, right?"

"What are you talking about?" I said, a little exasperated.

"You are becoming the incel now!"

"Shut up!" I screamed.

"It is true! You are involuntary celibate. You want so hard to get fucked by this guy, and he just doesn't want to."

"I don't know. Maybe he was sick, which is why he didn't attend class today."

"Come on. I have never seen him miss a class. No one has."

"Even if you are right, I am not an incel by any means!"

"Are you sure? How is it going with Professor Peck, then?"

At that moment, I hated my friend.

"Well, maybe I am going through a brief phase. But it is not like last time when I went for full weeks until I could get a good fuck."

"So, you are a recurring incel then."

"That is entirely untrue. I had a bad streak back then, and now I'm dealing with two idiots. But I have everything under control."

"We will see," she said and giggled.

I decided to try just one more time to get what I wanted. If Mark didn't take the bait, then I would move on. I didn't even like him that much. Not at all. In fact, I just wanted him to fuck me. It was that simple. The week following the Friday, he didn't attend class, he seemed nowhere to be found. We didn't cross paths in the hallways, and I was starting to accept that I might not see him again. And then Friday came, and even though I tried to arrive at class early, I could not do so because I got into another misadventure with a man (I won't go into great detail here because this is a story about Mark). I can only say that I barely made it to class when it was about to start. I walked in, limping from how hard I had just been fucked in the ass. So yes, I wasn't an incel at all.

I was extremely disheartened when I walked into the classroom because I didn't immediately spot Mark. But then I noticed that he was there; he wasn't sitting in his usual first row but rather in the third. There was an empty seat just to his side, so I took it without hesitation.

"Hi, Mark," I said. "I was wondering if we would ever meet again."

"What do you want with me?"

Okay, that really felt like an insult.

"You know what I want."

"B-but are you for real?"

"What do you think? Did you like the sight of my boobs?"

"I mean... you are the first woman ever to be interested in me. I worry you are just doing this to make fun of me after. Or maybe you have an ongoing bet with someone that you would seduce the ugly nerd in your Spanish class."

Given my ongoing silly turf with Julia, he wasn't entirely wrong about the bet. Still, he was wrong in thinking I could gain anything by finally fucking him.

"Still, here we are. Don't think I didn't notice what you did moving from the first row."

He didn't look back at me. Instead, he now again looked immersed in the class, as if nothing else existed besides him and the professor giving the lecture.

"So?"

"Shhhh... class has just started," he said.

I took a sheet of paper from my notebook and wrote:

"DO YOU WANT ME TO SUCK YOUR COCK?" I passed it to him, who took it, gave it a quick glance, and immediately flushed red.

The time for words was over. I groped with my right hand under the table until I reached his leg and moved slowly to his bulge that seemed like it was trying to escape from his pants. His face was red, and he was sweating.

"Has any woman ever touched you like this before?" I asked him in a whisper.

"NO!" he almost screamed.

"Very good, Mark! Muy bien!" said Professor Salazar. "The answer to the question is "No." The complete sentence is 'No, nunca me sucedió.' Which means 'No, that never happened to me.'"

Mark's dick was now fully erect. I started massaging it while, with my left hand, I went under my own pants, looking for my juicy pussy. I looked around to check that no one was seeing us. Our classmates seemed as bored as ever, but no one was looking our way. At least that I could tell.

I slid my hand under his pants and underwear. It was a nice, medium cock. Not too big, not too small, but hard as a rock it was. I grabbed it and started rubbing it.

"I will milk you dry. Do you want that?" I whispered in his ear while I continued rubbing his dick even harder. His face seemed like he was about to explode.

"SI," he said out loud.

"Si?" said professor Salazar. "Are you not feeling well then? I could tell by your face."

"No!" said Mark, trying to control himself from screaming in agonizing pleasure as I kept rubbing his cock as if there was no tomorrow. "I didn't want to answer that, professor. I am fine. Thank you for your concern."

Salazar looked at me, and I returned a smile. He then looked again at Mark before continuing with his class. He obviously suspected something odd was going on. Still, he did not know that my hands were busy, one with fingers well inside my wet pussy and the other going through all of Mark's mast.

"Put your pants down," I whispered.

"W-w-why?"

"You'll see."

He pulled off his pants and underwear. Now his cock was at large and unbounded.

My pussy started to contract, and I knew I was nearing the peak. I felt my legs tremble, and a rush of pleasure flew through my body. I had to bite my lips not to let out a scream of pleasure. Then, with the hand freed from rubbing my pussy, I picked up a pen, raised it to Mark's eyes, and dropped it on the floor next to him.

I then arched my back and acted as if I was going for it, but instead, I went straight for Mark's cock and put it in my mouth. I started sucking his crown with delicate licks before completely engulfing the rest of it. I went all the way until it completely landed in my throat and went forward and backward, playing with my tongue on his dick. I could sense how his body trembled that he was about to come, so I intensified the rhythm of my sucking, and he finally came in a large explosion of cum that filled my mouth. It was warm and tasty, and I swallowed it all.

"OHHHH" he screamed.

"Very well. That is the correct answer, Mark. To present different options in Spanish, we use the word 'O.' Like for example, in '¿Qué te gusta más? ¿La leche O el café?' Which translates as 'What do you prefer? Milk or coffee." Said Professor Salazar.

I returned to my seat and looked at Mark, who seemed completely relaxed.

"If you ask me, I prefer milk," I said to him and smiled, showcasing my cum-covered teeth.

The class was finishing just as we had. People started to grab their stuff and leave, and Mark simply said to me,

"Uh, thank you for that. I will not forget it."

"I know," I responded.

"So... I guess I will see you around?"

"Sure."

He left, and I stood alone, the last to leave. I was eager to tell Julia what had just happened, so I called her on my way back to my room.

"I did it!" I screamed at the phone, "I finally sucked Mark Bowden's cock!"

Julia let out a joyful cry.

"I can't believe you!"

I filled her in on the whole story, and she seemed genuinely interested in hearing it. Then, after I had finished speaking, she was silent for a moment.

"So? What do you think?" I asked her.

"Well, I am afraid I cannot accept that you beat me on my prediction."

"What are you talking about?"

"You said you would fuck the guy. I said you would not. You didn't."

"Are you deaf? What have I just told you?"

"You told me you sucked his cock and swallowed his cum. But you didn't fuck him."

"You bitch!" I screamed.

I knew, in the end, that she was right. And while she had prevailed this time, I would be the last to laugh. But that is a story for another time. Until then, warm kisses wherever you most want!

*You can check it here: My Sister's Boyfriend.

Pleasing My Professor

T he time has come for me to tell you about my taboo affair with my Political Science professor, Dr. Jeremy Peck, or "Pecker," as I like to call him, for reasons that will shortly become obvious.

I can say that I became obsessed with Peck the moment I first saw him: a tall, African-American guy with an ample and clean smile, short curly hair, and fit, muscled arms and torso that was easy to guess under the white, spotless tight-fitting shirt he always wore in class. It was like love at first sight, only that I would not say exactly "love" but an uncontrollable urge to feel his dick inside my pussy. I had never been with a black man before, but my friend Julia had. You need to know something about Julia: while she enjoys sex as much as I do, she is much more discreet with her affairs. She usually tells little about who she is fucking or has fucked recently. Moreover, she is much pickier than I am (Although that is simple since I'll fuck almost any guy I run into... as well as some girls, but that's a tale for another time!)So, when

Julia told me about the black man she had met on Tinder and how he had fucked her until exhaustion, I knew she really meant it.

"His dick," she said, gasping for air as if just remembering the guy's cock was giving her shudders in her vagina, "you had to see that monstrous dick. It was something I'd never seen before. Thick and harder than a piece of iron. He pumped my pussy with that thing like he was drilling gas from solid rock. I felt like I would not be able to walk normally after that. Of course, that didn't happen, but my god, was that one fuck to remember."

I heard my friend telling me about her experience and felt immediately jealous. I knew what they said about African-Americans having big, thick dicks. I had also seen some interracial porn where that was most clear. I immediately felt how a new fantasy formed in my mind: I wanted to be the white chick that gets fucked hard by a black man. I had only one big problem: I didn't know where to start looking for some good black dick. Not only I wanted a good thick black dick to fuck me, but I needed it to be from a mature guy. After fucking a ton of guys my age, I was starting to feel like I wanted to try a more mature guy. There is nothing particularly wrong with guys my age. I will fuck almost any guy who comes my way (except people with poor personal hygiene! That is the only thing I cannot stand!). Still, I was growing a little tired of the same old shenanigans. You know how it goes: you fuck a guy; he thinks he has fallen in love with you when in reality, he just wants to secure pussy for some time; things turn nasty when you tell him it was just a one-night stand. And that is the best scenario. The worst, and most common, is you fuck a guy, and he is just terrible at doing it. Men, I have learned, are like wines; the older they are, the better they get (at fucking.) So I wanted a black guy to fuck me, and I wanted him to be an older man so that I would not have to deal with all the "I love you" crap and to get to taste an experienced man.

Enter professor Peck. Do you want me to tell you I enrolled in his class because I was eager to learn Political Science? Do you think I care about Machiavelli and all those old white men who wrote about politics hundred years ago, or do you want me to tell you the truth? Well, I am not a liar. I knew he was a black man, that he doubled me in age, and that there were rumors about him having affairs with his students during office hours. So I didn't give it much thought and enrolled in his class. I attended the first class with the most provocative outfit I could wear without being expelled.

Given that I attended a small liberal arts college, I could carry some flashy cleavage, not for the faint of heart. As a proud carrier of 34 DD breasts, you can imagine how everything went. It was as if all the guys (and some gals) in college were suddenly aware of my existence. And I cannot blame them, as I really was something to see. So, I entered the classroom, sat in the first row, and waited patiently for the professor to arrive. And when he got there, he noticed me. That I can say. During the class, his eyes were fixated on my tits. He was talking and explaining, even moving around the classroom, yet his eyes would find their way to stare at my breasts. So, after the class finished and while he was picking up his stuff, I went straight to him and, playing dumb, told him I really had enjoyed his class. He blushed, and I could notice some sweat suddenly coming from the top of his head.

"Thank you," he said, walking towards the classroom door.

"professor, before you leave!" I said, intercepting him near the door as he got away, "all this seems so difficult for me. Would I be fine to drop by during your office hours?"

He took the palm of his hand to his forehead to dry some of the sweat.

"Well, of course. I mean, office hours are just for that. To help students. So yes. And now, if you excuse me, I need to get to another class," he said, leaving me standing there.

In the following weeks, I repeated the same act: I dressed as the slut I am, sat in the first row of his classes, and said something stupid to him at the end when everyone had left, and he was still collecting his belongings. During those weeks, he never lost his visible nervousness when I approached him, but he never looked back at my tits like during the first class. I felt slightly disappointed as things were not getting closer to where I was expecting. I then decided that I would need to move to attend his office hours. The persistent rumors on the campus stated he used to take pretty girls into his office and fuck them in the ass against his file cabinet. I had even heard it firsthand one day when in the washroom. That day, after lunch, I went to the bathroom to touch myself and keep my pussy happy. While doing this, I heard an exchange student, a Greek girl named Iliona Zervas, and one of her friends enter the bathroom. They stood before the mirror to touch their make-up when Iliona told about his experience with professor Peck.

"So, you know how I took this class last semester with the black guy?"

"Which class?"

"Political Science. The professor is this amazing middle-aged black guy."

"Yes, I think I know. But I am not sure."

"Oh, my god. You sure have seen him in the hallways. He is this fit, serious guy. He could be our dad. Gee, he even has a daughter our age! Anyway, the thing is that I took his class. It was tough, but I passed it just barely. One day, after I had finished the course, I decided to thank him personally in his office. I don't know why I had that thought. I was so thankful for him and all he had done for me. His was one of the first courses I took once I arrived. He had been extremely accommodating given that I barely knew how things are done here, used to how University is in Europe. So, one day when I had some free time during the afternoon, I remembered he had his office hours during that time, and so I went to thank him personally. I went into his office and told him I was thankful for everything he had done for me. Now, because this professor believes in being accessible to students, whenever you go to see him, he does not greet you behind a tall desk like any other professor but instead makes you sit directly in front of him, with nothing in between. It transforms the situation into a conversation between friends rather than a hierarchical one. So, to make things short, I was there, sitting in front of him, and I couldn't help but notice his crotch. I didn't intend at first, but it was just that it seemed so tight that my eyes couldn't get away from there. And I completely lost my train of thought. All the things I wanted to say to him and that I had prepared in my mind were suddenly completely gone, erased from my mind. He noticed it. 'Is everything right?' he asked me."

"And what did you say?"

"I don't know what went into my mind then because I told him I was getting distracted by his penis. I literally said that! Can you imagine?"

"OH MY GOSH! What happened then?"

"He smiled and said he was used to people getting hypnotized. I believe he used that word with his cock and balls. And then he stood up and came near me. I was still sitting there. I don't know what happened to me. I had never done something like that before. Still, it was as if I had suddenly become possessed by lust because, without giving it a second thought, my fingers went straight to his crotch. I gently massaged his dick over his pants. It got hard almost immediately. 'Continue,' he whispered, looking down at me from above. I was feeling excited. There I was, massaging the professor's balls and cock in his office. 'Yes, daddy,' I said. I don't know where I came from with that. It just felt correct. After all, as I told you, he has a daughter our age! So I then unzipped his pants and put them down. He was wearing a slip. His cock was so huge that it seemed to be trying to escape its confinement. I was amazed and felt scorching right then. I wanted to see with my own eyes that penis. I needed to have it in my hand. I pulled his slip down, and then there it was. A monstrous, black, venous member like I had never seen before. I grabbed it with my hand, which was tiny in comparison. I needed my two hands to get to a little more than half the mast's length. I massaged it and felt it in my hand. It was pulsing, getting bigger by the second. He grabbed me by the head with one hand he grabbed his cock. He started slapping me in the face with it. 'Have you seen one like this before? I am sure you don't have black cock in Greece, do you?' I told him I had never seen a black man's dick before, and he told me, 'Well, you are learning how it is now. You will learn the hard way.' I was feeling absolutely delighted. I never expected to end up having the professor's cock slapping me in the face when I went there, but I was loving it either way. 'Suck it,' he said. I was unsure. I had barely sucked dick before, and this one looked so monstrous that I felt afraid I could not take it all."

"This is so hot. I would have never imagined that professor Peck would do that."

"Yes, I know. Me neither. I took it into my mouth and licked the crown. It was bittersweet and a little rough. I loved it. And I loved how his eyes went immediately looking for the ceiling. I could tell he was enjoying it, which turned me on even more. I took it out of my mouth and stood in front of him. 'What?' he said. And so I told him I wanted to feel it inside my pussy. He smiled. It was this sensual smile that left all his pearl-like teeth uncovered. His lips looked thicker, aroused. 'Turn your back on me,' he said, and I complied. 'Put your pants down,' he ordered. 'Yes, professor,' I said. He pushed me in the back until I reached a filing cabinet. He made me lean against it. Then I heard how he spat his hand and brushed his dick with it. I felt his big, delicate hands on my back, pushing until my body arched. Then, he gently kicked my legs so that I spread them. 'Do you want to get fucked in the ass?' he asked me. I told him yes, whatever my black daddy wanted, I also wanted. So then I felt how he went inside me with a single, powerful push. I let go of a painful scream. His hand covered my mouth as he pushed his cock inside my ass. It was so massive I felt like I was about to die of pleasure. With his other hand, he searched for my clit and rubbed it with an ability I have never experienced before."

"Older guys are the best."

"The absolute best. They know how things work, how to move, how to give a woman a good fuck!"

"I am feeling so horny right now. "

"I know. I was as well. He pumped my ass for a few minutes more. With each thrust of his massive cock inside, my legs trembled. It was insane. And incredibly pleasurable. I could sense how he was approaching his orgasm, and I was also coming. A few more strokes, and he dumped this massive load of scum into my ass. I have never felt something like that before. My clit was on fire. He rubbed even harder, and I came just as he pulled his dick out. His dense cum dripped onto the carpeted office floor like olive oil. I have never in my life seen so much jizz."

"Wow, that is such an amazing story. So, what happened next? Did you see him again?"

"After we finished, he put on his clothes and commanded me to do the same. 'I am grateful that you came here to thank me for the class you took with me,' he told me. Obviously, I was the thankful one. Not only had he been an amazing professor who had taught me Political Science, but now he had become my professor in anal. I will never forget that afternoon in his office. As for a continued commitment, no. That was the only time we fucked. After that, we crossed paths several times in the hallways, but he ignored me. I don't know why. I tried going to his office hours a few more times but couldn't find him in his office. I also tried emailing him, but he never responded. I don't know. Maybe it was something that belonged to that moment only. I have more or less accepted it."

The Greek girl and her friend finished fixing their make-up and left the washroom. I took a few more minutes before leaving, as what I had just heard had turned me on. I touched myself, dreaming of professor Peck-er's big thick black cock destroying my pussy, and came to a quick orgasm. At first, I felt relieved, but then I realized I really needed to get fucked in the ass by my professor.

And then, nothing was happening. I attended class after class, dressing more and more like a total whore, and while I was getting the attention of some losers in my class, I was not getting the professor's eyes, which was my primary goal.

"I can't believe this is happening!" I told my friend Julia during one of our lunches together at the college's cafeteria.

"Why are you so obsessed with him? Move over! There is plenty of dick out there!"

"You don't understand. You didn't hear what I heard."

"You mean the story about the Greek girl you overheard in the washroom?"

"That one," I said, sipping my Diet Coke.

"And how do you know it is even real?"

"You think she could fake it?"

"I mean... you weren't there. You just heard the woman tell the story. As far as I know, she could have been boasting for clout. Who knows?!"

"I don't think such a story could be faked. It had a lot of details."

"Yes, particularly her comparison of his cum to olive oil," said Julia, rolling her eyes.

"Well, she is Greek, after all! Isn't she?"

"So what? Did she fuck him or make a salad?"

"You are so rude!"

"Forget him. Move over. You still have to prove that you can get to fuck Mark, the virgin."

You, my dear reader, will remember how that story ended*, so I will not indulge in telling it again here, so we don't get distracted.

I decided I needed to take the matter to the next level. So I attended professor Peck's office hours the following week. If what the Greek girl told her friend was true, then I also had to take my chance. I decided on a modest outfit that afternoon. Well, modest compared to what I was used to taking to class. It was still pretty, but it left much more to the imagination. I first emailed him to ensure he would be at his office, telling him I wanted to consult with him for the incoming test. He promptly answered that he would gladly receive me in his office. I sensed things had started to move in the correct direction once again.

And so I went to his office. I knocked on the door, opened and found him typing on his laptop.

"Miss Luna, nice to see you here," he said, getting up from behind his desk, "please, take a seat. What can I do for you?"

I sat in the chair he had pointed at, and he sat in another one just in front of me, his legs crossed. It was as Ilona had told her friend that afternoon in the washroom. I thought that was another promising development, and my pussy immediately got wet. Even more, after seeing by myself how professor's bulge became so notorious in that position.

He stared at me.

"So? How can I help you?"

I mumbled some words. I had nothing to talk to him about except how much I desired to get fucked by his fat, black cock.

"I think... I have lost my train of thought," I finally said, sticking my eyes to his groin.

"I see," he said pensively "well, Miss Luna... If you cannot think of anything you would like to ask or consult with me, I will ask you to leave because I need to finish some grading."

I didn't know what to answer. I had expected him to lead the way, and now he had just invited me to leave.

I stood up, and he did the same. I approached him while he stood motionless.

"I think you know why I came here," I said.

I could sense how he had started to sweat.

"I do. And it is for this reason, Miss Luna, I must politely request you to leave my office once again."

"What is the problem? You only fuck your Greek students? I have Hispanic heritage. Don't you like that?"

I could see how his Adam's apple moved as he gulped.

"Please, Miss Luna. I don't know what you suggest, but I am currently your professor. So whatever you are thinking, I cannot allow it to happen."

I stretched my arm and reached for his balls under the pants. His cock had awakened and was getting harder by the second.

"I think your balls and dick would beg to disagree."

He stood stiff in his place without moving a muscle.

"Please, Miss Luna. This is highly inappropriate."

"I saw how you looked at my tits during our first class. And then, in the following classes, you didn't. What happened?"

"Please, leave now, or I will have to file a complaint against you. And I really would rather not."

"Don't you want to push your hard black cock into my tight ass?"

He blinked. I squeezed his balls a little more.

"I... I can't. You are my student, and this would not be appropriate. I could get into a lot of trouble."

"You already are in a lot of trouble, professor. I assume, for the ring you carry on your left hand, that there is a Mrs. Peck that would not want to know that her husband fucks his students right in their ass in his office. I am right?"

"Just leave. And don't come back," he said. "I will pretend this never happened. But you have to promise me to stop your little seduction game."

"You disappointed me, professor," I said, leaving his office.

I was genuinely disappointed. I had had my high hopes of getting my ass ripped by a black cock, and instead, I had been humiliated with a refusal. I had been reBUTTed when all I had wanted was to get my BUTT filled with black cock.

I decided I would not tell Julia about my failure. She was having a lot of fun at my expense with all the things going on with Mark, the virgin, and I didn't want her to have even more reasons to make fun of me.

Next class, I attended wearing simple clothes. I wasn't really in the mood to push things even further. professor Peck did as if I wasn't there, and I, for once, listened to his boring class. I had spent all the previous classes just imagining how I would get my ass ripped by his black mamba and hadn't really given any attention to his explanations. Now I was overwhelmed by his explanations, unable to gasp at anything he said. I needed to pass his class! I came home that night feeling depressed and discouraged. The final test was approaching fast. I decided I was going to pass that class, whatever it took. It was not only that I needed it for my degree, but now it had become a pride thing. I would not allow professor Peck to humiliate me with a failing grade, not after how he had humiliated me in his office. So, I dedicated most of my time to studying for the following weeks. I stopped going out on Friday and Saturday nights; I stopped fucking random guys; I was unrecognizable. I was also feeling like shit. My libido was through the roof, and while I spent much of it reading and studying, I had to go to great distances to keep my pussy from rebelling. I knew that if I indulged in self-pleasure or, worse, a single fuck with a guy, I would undo all of my hard work and never be able to study again.

The day of the final test came, and I put myself entirely on it. I did my best. Nevertheless, when the allotted time to complete it ended, I was still writing my final answer. I handed my test with a mix of feelings. I knew I had done my very best. For another thing, I was pretty sure it would not have been enough for me to pass the class. To pass, I needed to get a high score on the test to compensate for doing almost nothing else during the rest of the class.

I tried to move on and not think much about the situation during the following days. A little more than a week later, on a Friday morning, I received an email from professor Peck. It was short and sober, and he asked me to see him at his office the same day to discuss my final grade. I read his email several times. Each time I read it, I grew angrier. It seemed like he hadn't humiliated me enough, and he just wanted to keep humiliating me! That was why he was calling me to his office? I decided that if that was the case, I would make things difficult for him. I put up tight leggings that showed my butt and a shirt with a cleavage that left little to the imagination. If professor Peck wanted to play hard, I would play harder.

I arrived at the convened time, knocked on the door, and heard him calling me from the inside: "Come in, please. And make sure to close the door behind you."

He was sitting in the chair behind his desk and made no attempt to move.

"Please, take a seat," he told me.

"Won't you come and face me?" I asked.

"I am facing you, Miss Luna."

"I mean, without the intrusion of your desk."

"I will feel more comfortable having this conversation like this."

"Fine," I conceded and sat on the chair he had pointed to me.

"So, Miss Luna...," he began, "I wanted to talk to you regarding your test."

"Here it comes," I said.

"Excuse me?"

"Come on, say what we already know: I failed the class. It is fine. I mean... I did my best, but it was not enough."

"Oh, no. On the contrary. You passed the test and the class. I wanted to tell you in person. I am pleasantly surprised, I might say. There was a clear change of gears in your attitude towards this class after... our last meeting. And so, I wanted to congratulate you."

He extended me my graded test. It said I had got just the grade I needed to pass the class. I felt relieved and a little disappointed as well. I had attended the meeting expecting a fight and was handed a passing grade instead. What was next? A tap on my shoulder?

"Well, thank you, professor. I am sorry about what happened here the last time and...."

"Forget it. All is fine."

I stood up, and he did the same.

"So, well, I suppose that this is it, then. Is there anything else you wanted to tell me?" I asked.

He smiled. It was a deep, almost scary smile.

"Miss Luna, you should know that I am still your professor. I mean, you finished the course, and everything is done, but I can still change your test grade for the time being."

"Is this some kind of threat? I don't understand your point, professor Peck."

"No threat. It is just something I like my special students to remember. I did you a little favor, don't you think? I mean, with your grade. You tried your best to pass the course, but I could still lower your final grade and have a good justification for doing it."

He walked towards me.

"You wouldn't do that, would you?"

"I certainly would prefer not to have. But, you know, I got a little sour taste in my mouth after our last meeting," he said, grabbing my hand and putting it on his groin. His dick was hard as a hammer.

"Now, take off your clothes, Miss. I want to see that blushing ass of yours," he said.

I did as he told me and got completely naked.

"Is this what you wanted?"

"Shut up and obey," he said.

"Why now and not then?"

"Things will be done as I please. And you are going to shut the fuck up, little slut. Who do you think you are? Coming to my office, grabbing my balls as you, please? You thought that by doing that, I would give you a passing grade? Now you are going to see how things go with me."

"I will do as you please, professor."

"I bet you will," he said, pulling down his pants and underwear.

There it was, a big, fat black cock the length of my arm. I shuddered at the idea of getting pounded by that monstrosity.

"You like what you see, Miss Luna?"

I nodded.

"You are suddenly silent. What happened to the disrespectful brat who would come to this office and brag about doing what she wanted?"

He slapped me on the ass with his enormous hands. I felt a mix of pain and pleasure. My pussy was getting inundated with juice.

"I see you have a nice ass. I certainly wouldn't mind fucking it. Have you ever been fucked in the ass before, little brat?"

"Not by a black cock like yours, professor."

"Ah, I see," he said, slapping me again, in the tits this time, and much harder than before. My white skin turned red in the shape of his hand.

"Open your legs," he ordered.

I complied. He went to my back and got to his knees.

"You will stay quiet. Understood? You will fail this class if you move or do anything I didn't ask. I am clear?"

"Yes, professor,"

I sensed the tip of his tongue going through my calves, slowly climbing to my asshole. His tongue entered my hole completely and licked me like a pomegranate. I felt like melting inside out. My legs were trembling, and I hardly could manage to stay on my feet, but I knew I could not move as the professor had not given me permission. He slipped one finger into my pussy. It entered with ease; I was soaking wet. He continued licking my ass while he massaged my pussy with his hand. I felt like I would come any second, but then he got up and pushed me from the back into the file cabinet.

"Now, I will fuck your ass. And you will like it. If I hear you let a single scream of pain, you will immediately fail this class. Is it clear?"

"Yes, professor," I said, and as soon as I finished saying that, his fat shaft got into my ass in a single, violent pump. The pain was almost unbearable. I had never experienced such a big cock in my ass. It felt like it was going to get through my insides. I could sense his agitated breathing right behind my left ear. His perfume, which said "professor" in all its delicate fragrance, was mixed with an almost animal scent of sex and sweat.

"How does this feel, Miss Luna? Did you really think that you could play with me?"

I let out a little moan, and professor Peck slapped me in the ass with fury.

"What did I say? You will not do or say anything I don't specifically allow you."

"Yes, professor."

He continued drilling my ass with his hard cock.

"So, what do you say? You thought you could play me?"

"Yes."

"Yes, what?"

"Yes, professor."

"That is better. And are you sorry about thinking you could trick me?"

"Yes, professor."

"You are such a fucking slut!" he said to my ear, "and I will fill your ass with so much cum, you will need days to clean it all up! Do you want that?"

"Yes, professor,"

My ass was being destroyed. It felt delicious. He then moved his hand back to my pussy and started to move his long, thin fingers with an ability I had never seen before in another man. He truly knew how to give pleasure to a woman.

"Do you like it, Miss Luna?"

"Yes, professor."

"What do you like more?"

"I like you are older than me. You know how to please a woman. And such a big black cock as yours is something I have never experienced before."

He let out a savage scream in my ear. His dick trembled inside my ass, and I immediately felt his warm jam filling my butt. Then, with a renewed push, his fingers rubbed my clit, and I couldn't help but bend my body as a big orgasm started from my ass, where his dick was still palpitating inside to my other limbs.

He then took his cock out, and my ass started dripping with his never-ending load of cum. I thought he was right and that I would probably drip it for days. Such was the immensity of what he had deposited there.

"Now get dressed and get out of here. I don't want to see you ever again near here."

"Yes, professor," I said timidly.

After getting dressed, I walked out of the office. He had won. He had successfully played me. For once in a long time, I had not ended with the upper hand. Even so, that had been precisely what I had been looking for: an older black man that could give me a fuck in the ass that I would never forget. In that sense, I had also won.

So that is it! That is the story about how I got my ass destroyed by the hard, fat black cock of professor Peck-er during college. Until the next time, warm kisses wherever you most want!

*You can check it here: My oral test

Also By Ashley Dixon

After learning about the crazy, steamy times her friend Rebecca had during her recent trip to Argentina, Erin Luna, our insatiable protagonist, decides that she also wants a taste of the world-famous "Argentinian meat." And so she books a trip South, and that is when things turn spicy. During her stay, she will learn an unconventional way of

dancing the tango - with four enthusiastic soccer players eager to show
her why the country is known for its passionate culture.
And for Erin, who lives by the maxim "Travel the world, f* the globe!"
things couldn't get any better.
Contains: Reverse harem, MMMF, Oral and much more.